Tumbler
and the Slippery Ice

Illustrations by Craig Cameron

EGMONT

EGMONT

We bring stories to life

First published in Great Britain 2010
by Egmont UK Limited,
239 Kensington High Street, London W8 6SA

Based on the television series Bob the Builder
© 2010 HIT Entertainment Limited and Keith Chapman. All rights reserved.
The Bob the Builder name and character, related characters and riveted logo
are trademarks of HIT Entertainment Limited.

HiT entertainment

ISBN 978 1 4052 5349 9

1 3 5 7 9 10 8 6 4 2

Printed in Italy

FSC

Mixed Sources
Product group from well-managed
forests and other controlled sources

Cert no. TT-COC-002332
www.fsc.org
© 1996 Forest Stewardship Council

Egmont is passionate about helping to preserve the world's remaining ancient forests.
We only use paper from legal and sustainable forest sources.

This book is made from paper certified by the Forestry Stewardship Council (FSC),
an organisation dedicated to promoting responsible management of forest resources.
For more information on the FSC, please visit www.fsc.org. To learn more about
Egmont's sustainable paper policy, please visit www.egmont.co.uk/ethical

Tumbler is excited about a new ice rink being built in Bobland Bay. But will he overcome his fear of the ice before the rink is finished?

It was a cold, snowy day in Sunflower Valley. The team huddled together for warmth as Bob told them about their special new job.

"We're going to be building the Bobland Bay ice rink today!" said Bob.

"Ooh, how exciting!" said the team.

"I love ice-skating," said Dizzy, and she did a fancy spin on the frozen ground.

"I'll skate with you, Dizzy," said Tumbler. "I'm sure it can't be that hard!"

Bob asked Dizzy and Tumbler to fetch some special lime concrete for the base. Then he told the team they would be using recycled wood to make the seats.

"Reduce, reuse, recycle!" the machine team cheered.

As Dizzy and Tumbler set off for the builder's yard to fetch the lime concrete, Bob and Wendy marked out the area where the rink would be built. Then Muck and Scoop dug out the base.

Lofty fetched wood for the side panels, and Wendy unpacked the refrigeration unit that would freeze water into ice.

Dizzy and Tumbler rolled through the snow towards the yard.

"Look, ice!" cried Dizzy. She raced onto a patch of ice and began to twirl.

"That's easy! Watch this," said Tumbler. He followed Dizzy and tried to copy her moves.

But Tumbler had never skated before and he began to slip and slide on the ice.

"Whoaaah!" Tumbler wailed, and he skidded off the ice and into a bush!

"Tumbler! Are you OK?" Dizzy asked.

"Er, yes, fine, thanks," Tumbler said, shakily.

"This way to the yard, then," sang Dizzy, sliding back across the ice.

But Tumbler was worried. The ice was very slippery!

"I'm a bit scared of the ice now," Tumbler told two friendly squirrels, "but I don't want Dizzy to know!"

"Come on, slowcoach!" shouted Dizzy.

"Er, Dizzy, I think we should go this way instead," Tumbler trembled. He rolled towards a road that led away from the ice. "There are more squirrels to see!"

"OK," said Dizzy, "but I hope it doesn't make us late."

The road took Tumbler and Dizzy a long way from the yard.

"I'm not sure we're going the right way," said Dizzy, "but you have found more ice!" She twirled neatly on the shiny patch.

"I wish I could skate," sighed Tumbler to himself. "Dizzy, I want to go a different way," he said. "That road is too bumpy."

"OK," said Dizzy, frowning, "but we are getting further from the yard, you know!"

Soon, the two machines were speeding through the snowy valley.

"Don't go too fast," cried Dizzy. "These roads are very slippery!"

Suddenly they came to a wide patch of ice. Tumbler braked, but Dizzy couldn't stop. She skidded on the ice and landed with a bump in a snowdrift. She was stuck!

Tumbler felt helpless. How was he going to help Dizzy if he couldn't skate?

"Tumbler, come and push me out of this snow!" said Dizzy.

"I can't!" cried Tumbler. "I'm scared to go on the ice. I feel so silly," he said, sadly.

"You're not silly!" laughed Dizzy. "You just need to learn how to skate. Go slowly to start with, then glide."

So Tumbler shuffled on to the ice. He skidded at first then found his balance. He glided over to Dizzy and pushed her free!

Soon, Dizzy and Tumbler were dashing through the snow to the builder's yard.

They collected the concrete, then hurried back to the skate park.

Bob was very pleased to see Dizzy and Tumbler. Now the concrete could be poured onto the rink.

"We need to let the concrete set, then we'll fill the rink with water and freeze it into ice!" Bob explained.

By the next evening, the rink was ready and all of Bobland Bay wanted to try it out!

"Who's going to have the first skate?" asked Bob.

"Tumbler will!" squealed Dizzy, proudly.

But Tumbler was still nervous about going on the ice.

"Don't worry," Dizzy whispered to him. "Go slowly to start with, then glide."

"Slowly to start with, then glide," Tumbler repeated to himself, sliding out onto the ice. He soon found his balance and skated happily away.

"Well done, Tumbler," cheered Bob. "You're a brilliant skater for such a big strong machine!"

Tumbler beamed proudly. "It's easy when you know how," he smiled.

Start collecting your Bob the Builder Story Library NOW!

RRP £2.99

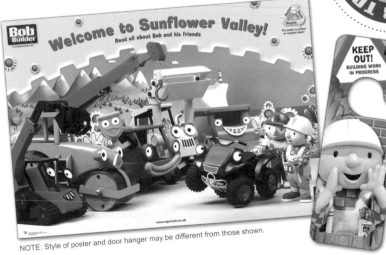

'Bob Goodies Please' Reply Card

Yes I have enclosed 4 special Bob Tokens so please send me a FREE Bob the Builder poster and door hanger ☒ (tick here)

Simply fill in your details below and send this page to:
BOB OFFERS, PO BOX 715, HORSHAM RH12 5WG

To be completed by an adult

Fan's name:

Address:

Postcode:

Email:

Date of birth:

Name of parent / guardian:

Signature of parent / guardian:

Please allow 28 days for delivery. Offer is only available while stocks last. We reserve the right to change the terms of this offer at any time. This does not affect your statutory rights. Offers apply to UK only.

We may occasionally wish to send you information about other Egmont children's books and updates from HIT Entertainment on Bob the Builder. If you would rather we didn't, please tick. ☒

Bob the Builder

Ref: BOB 006